LOFTS

BY JEFFREY WEISS

Photography by Jon Elliott and David Leach

W·W·NORTON & COMPANY
New York   London

Design: Alix Serniak
Illustrations: Ken Druse
Cover photo: Jon Elliott
Additional photographs by Suki Hill, J. Michael Kanouff,
Jeffrey Weiss, Nancy Tobie, Nick Gunderson

In addition to those whose homes are noted in the identifying
credits at the back of the book, I wish to thank the many generous
people who helped in the making of LOFTS. Foremost is my editor,
Ed Barber. As an editor I know how easy it is to obstruct and how
difficult it is to facilitate. Ed facilitates. I am especially grateful to:
Carla Cousins, Jeanne Diao, Tom and Jane Doyle, Lila Gault,
Joyce Goldstein, Betsy Groban, Trudy Kramer, John Loring, Karen
McCreedy, Jim Roper, Peter Stamberg, and Barbara Toll.

First Edition

Library of Congress Cataloging in Publication Data

Weiss, Jeffrey.
        Lofts.

        1.   Dwellings — United States.   2.   Buildings —
United States — Remodeling for other use.
I.   Title.
NA7208.F7   1979   728.3'1   79–13371
ISBN 0–393–01291–5
ISBN 0–393–00945–9 pbk.

1 2 3 4 5 6 7 8 9 0

For Yolande, Nina, and Nicholas

All over America our architectural heritage is being rediscovered and revived. Whole areas of the inner city — sometimes so close to decay and demolition that their disappearance seemed ordained — have come back to life in a splendid burst of artistic and commercial vitality. LOFTS is a visual celebration of the marvelous new residential uses that urban pioneers have found for the neglected and sometimes abandoned commercial buildings and grand old houses of the cities. The loft phenomenon is not confined to the giant cities, conversions and restorations are taking place in many small towns here and abroad. Whole sections of the London waterfront, strange old buildings in Paris, even granaries and mill sites throughout the South have been transformed. This book is a glimpse into the homes of those who have made successful attempts to personalize their living spaces.

What is a loft? Norval White, in THE ARCHITECTURE BOOK, defines lofts as "... the empty or simple attic spaces of architecture that allow happenings by default ... an urban loft ... is the high, open-spaced, many floored place of storage, industry, art and dwelling — untailored,

raw, and usable, in theory, for anything." Lofts allow their users the great luxury of enormous space — a monumental canvas on which to paint a real house. Sometimes the space comes complete with old detail: ornately decorated cast-iron interior pillars, filigreed plaster molding, magnificent maple floors. Sometimes it is truly raw space, and space that has to be cleared of years of debris as well. What follows is my idiosyncratic catalog of possibilities, a catalog that displays the results of what hearty applications of imagination, taste, effort, and, of course, money allow when applied to lofts.

The most well-known loft area in the country is Soho in lower Manhattan. That it is a neighborhood called by name is a tribute to the intrepid artists who began homesteading there after many small businesses had left the area. It also is a testament to the acumen of real estate speculators who know that naming a neighborhood is often equivalent to revalu-

ing it upward. Soho was once the exclusive preserve of light industry and warehousing. In 1971, however, the forty-three city blocks that comprise the area were designated as "legal" for mixed commercial and residential use, provided the residential users were officially certified by the city as "artists in need of large working space." No one seemed to anticipate the boom that followed. The huge-windowed, embellished cast-iron façade and the soaring ceilings of the 1870s have become the chic renovated residences of the 1970s. As often happens, artists seeking cheap rents led the way. They traded labor and art work for sinks and stoves. The dimensions of the lofts, often spaces of 4,500 to 8,500 square feet, the quality of light on all four sides through 8 or 10 foot high windows, and reinforced floors that enable massive sculpting and construction are not uncommon. And in the beginning it was cheap! The early loft pioneers did little more than install rudimentary plumbing and cooking facilities. Artists frequently are driven to treat their homes as another arena of artistic expression and their lofts soon took on a more ingenious and finished character. Once the ground was broken and the possibilities of spacious living made manifest, many nonartists flocked to the neighborhood. Now Soho is a full-scale residential community with hundreds of buildings that have been fully renovated. There is a large movement to cooperative ownership of those buildings, which unfortunately, sometimes prices them beyond the reach of artists who aspire to ownership. The movement has spread uptown and downtown in Manhattan — office buildings are

being converted into loft-apartments at a fantastic rate, and across the river in Brooklyn, the old navy yard and its environs are undergoing a similar transformation. The trend is countrywide. In Seattle, at Pike Market, old produce and fish warehouses have metamorphosed into galleries, shops, and lofts. In San Francisco and Sausalito, the incredible buildings in which the Liberty ships were fabricated during World War II now house people launching families and careers. In Boston, Cambridge, and Memphis, the interior walls of grand old mansions have been removed to revitalize the space for today's style. In all these places, and in many smaller towns as well, the freedom to find new and beautiful design solutions while keeping the exterior structures intact creates as special excitement. Bathrooms become sensual, warm, and sybaritic retreats, or ultramodern space-age fantasies; kitchens range from glossy high-tech functional to vivid recreations of down-home country style; living rooms, workrooms, and bedrooms all reflect their occupants' openness to unself-conscious personal design not often seen in their suburban counterparts. Collections of valuable art can be exhibited in a museumlike

setting or a whimsical array of old telephones can extend over thirty feet of wall space. Dramatic stairways spiral up to roof gardens, down to darkrooms or studios. Beams, brick, even the plumbing pipes, become decorative elements. Color and texture are present in abundance.

Each loft has the unique character and vitality of its occupants and I have tried to give the feeling of their homes through the many detail shots that are interspersed in the book. LOFTS, I hope, continues the task I set for myself in MADE WITH OAK, LIVING PLACES, and GOOD LIVES — to document in an informal and pleasurable way the infinite variety in the ways people of taste and style and some means choose to live. Scores of ideas are here for those interested in changing their own homes, or just in taking simple delight in the imaginative, beautiful, and even zany transformations that make loft living the premier urban architectural and design challenge of the last quarter of our century.

Jeffrey Weiss

2

3

4

5

6

8

9

11

12

13

14

16

17

18

19

21

22

23

24

25

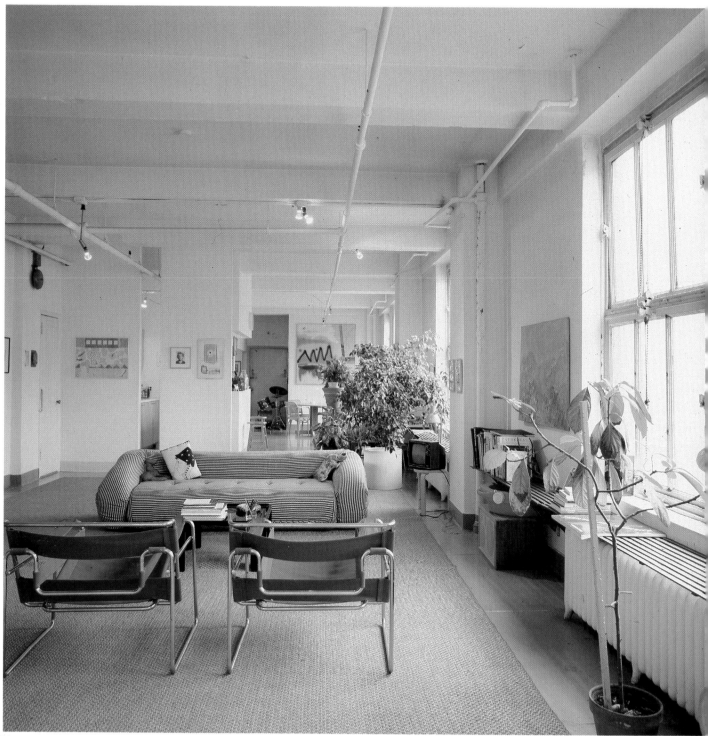

27

28

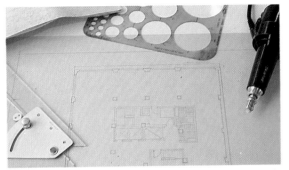

29

32

33

34

35

36

37

39

42

43

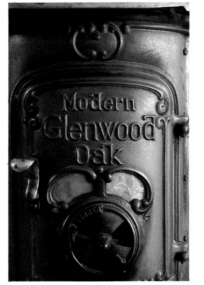

44

45

47

48

49

50

51

52

53

54

57

58

59

60

63

64

69

70

71

72

73

74

75

76

77

78

81

82

83

85

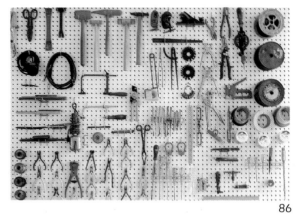

86

87

88

89

90

92

93

95

96

97

98

99

100

101

104

105

107

108

109

110

111

114

115

116

117

119

120

122

123

124

125

126

127

128

129

130

131

133

134

135

136

138

139

140

142

143

145

147

148

Photo Credits